Farmer Bob

Goes Surfing

OCEANS

FARMER BOB™

EDUCATION FLYING RHINOCEROS

Mailing Address: P.O. Box 3989
                     Portland, Oregon, U.S.A.
                     97208-3989

Email Address: bigfan@flyingrhino.com

Library of Congress Control Number:
2001135400

ISBN 1-883772-61-3
ISBN 1-883772-78-8 Farmer Bob Oceans series

Printed in Mexico

Farmer Bob works hard all day
to tend the soil and turf.
But when it's time to take a break
he just can't wait to surf.

The animals need vacations, too.
So, Bob piles them in his van.
Now they can warm themselves with sun
and frolic in the sand.

What would it be like
to swim beneath the sea,
exploring great kelp forests,
touching sea anemones?

Kelp Me!

Kelp is a kind of seaweed. There are many kinds of kelp. Some are very big. Giant kelp can grow to be 100 feet tall!

Kelp Aplenty

A lot of kelp growing in one place can form a kelp forest. Kelp forests are found in cold water, close to the coast.

Lying on his surfboard,
Bob paddles through the waves,
imagining what lies below:
strange fish and ocean caves.

Anemone Enemy

Some people think sea anemones look like flowers. They are actually animals. Most sea anemones attach to hard surfaces like rocks. They wait for fish or other prey to swim by. Some only eat tiny plankton. Stinging cells on their tentacles help them catch their prey.

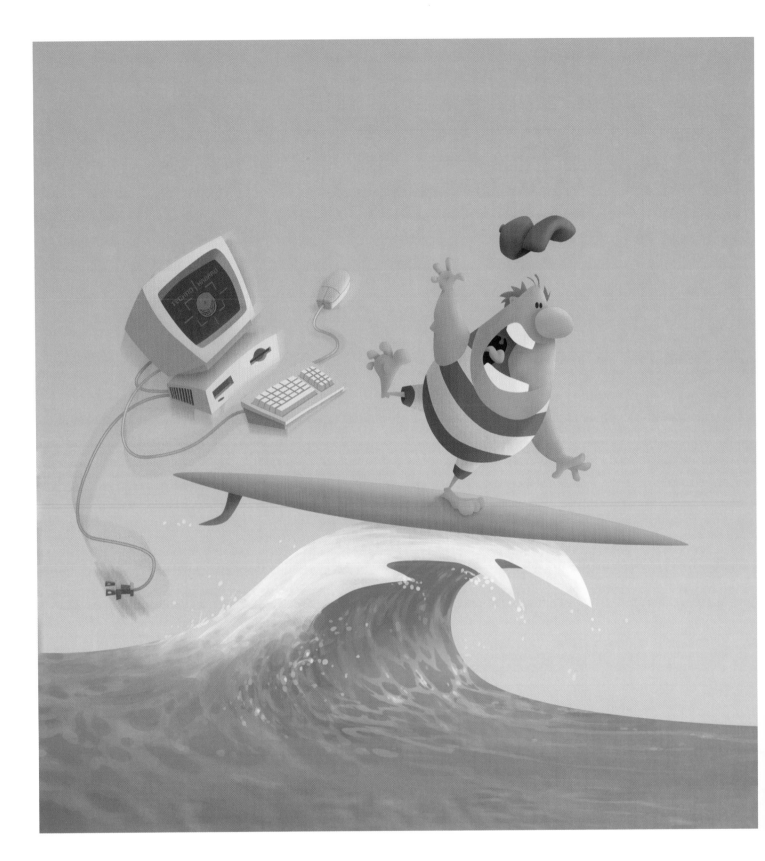

Splash!
Waves break when they reach the shore. This is called surf.

Surf's Up!
People have surfed for thousands of years. The first surfers lived on ocean islands. Some of the best surfing waves are found near islands.

Surfing is like balancing
on a board that won't stand still,
while all the time you're sliding
down a steep and slippery hill.

The only surfing Bob has done
is on the Internet.
But after wiping out nine times,
he tells himself, "No sweat."

Wild Wave Riders

Many surfers like big waves.
Some can surf waves that are
as tall as telephone poles!

Making Waves

Wind makes the waves on the ocean
surface. The size of the waves depends
on how strong the wind is.

But even Farmer Bob
wasn't ready for what came:
a wave so big and tall
it was impossible to tame.

Breathing Under Water

Fish need oxygen just like people do. They breathe through gills that take oxygen out of the water.

Scuba Tube

People can use air tanks to breathe under the water. Scuba divers wear air tanks on their backs. A tube brings air to the diver's mouth.

One minute Bob was riding,
serene atop the ocean.
Next, he was beneath the sea,
tumbling in slow motion.

Though he didn't quite know how,
Bob was breathing like sea creatures.
He found himself surrounded by
a school without a teacher.

Attention Class

Many fish swim in groups called schools. Fish that swim in schools can confuse predators.

Stay in School

Fish have special sensors on their heads and sides. The sensors feel motion in the water. This helps fish in a school tell where the other fish are swimming. This also helps the school stay together.

It was strange for Farmer Bob
to find himself in class
with fish instead of children,
including some sea bass.

Big Bad Bass

Some sea bass are very small and some are very big. The giant sea bass can be almost 7 feet long. It can weigh more than 500 pounds!

Proud Papa

Like most other fish, sea horses hatch from eggs. Female sea horses lay the eggs. Male sea horses carry the eggs until they hatch.

Some members of the class
were sea horsing around,
while others, like the clownfish,
were acting like class clown.

Sea Horsing Around
Sea horses can grab onto
things with their tails.

Where's the Circus?
A clownfish is a kind of anemone fish. Anemone fish live safely with sea anemones. Sea anemones' stinging cells do not hurt anemone fish.

11

A lecture was just starting
on the differences between
animals that live on land
and those that are marine.

The first creature that they looked at
was called a manatee.
It was also known as a "sea cow,"
Farmer Bob could plainly see.

Sea Cow Stats

Manatees are mammals. They don't really look like cows. They eat plants, such as sea grasses, like cows do. Full-grown manatees are about 10 feet long.

Listen to the Ocean

It is often too dark to see under the water. Dolphins use sound to find their way like bats do. Dolphins have great hearing.

None of this was news to Bob,
and so he swam away
to visit with some dolphins
that were frolicking at play.

Dolphin Symphony

Dolphins make two main types of sounds. They make clicking sounds to find their way in the ocean. They make whistle sounds, or squeals, to talk to other dolphins.

Bob tried to catch a dolphin.
He yelled, "Wait up, Mrs. Fish!"
"I'm a mammal, just like you," she said,
and gave her tail a swish.

"We're related to the whales.
We swim in groups called pods.
Our lungs breathe air, we birth live young.
We're nothing like a cod."

Hot and Cold

Dolphins and whales are mammals. Mammals are warm-blooded. Marine mammals have a thick layer of fat to help them stay warm.

Whale of a Tooth

There are two main types of whales: baleen and toothed whales. Baleen whales don't have teeth. They have strainers in their mouths called baleen.

"If you want to see strange critters
that will provide a treat,
swim deep down to the thermal vents.
Just don't expect much heat."

Mammals vs. Fish

Most mammal babies are born live. They drink their mother's milk for food. Most fish hatch from eggs. Young fish do not nurse from their mother. Fish are cold-blooded.

Take a Deep Breath

Mammals can't breathe under the water. They must swim to the surface to fill their lungs with air.

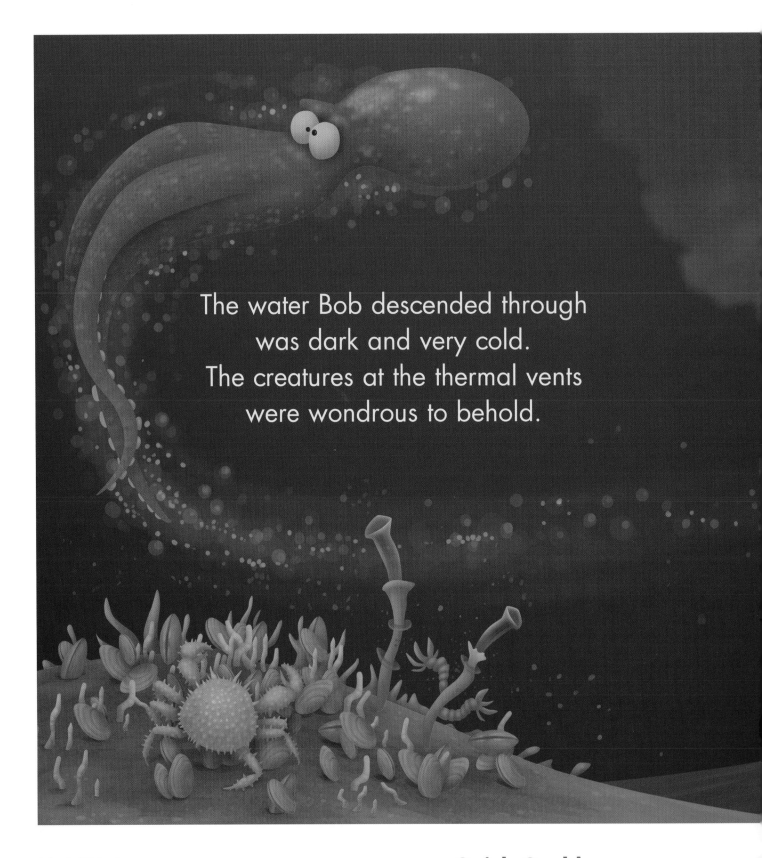

The water Bob descended through
was dark and very cold.
The creatures at the thermal vents
were wondrous to behold.

Hot Water . . .

Thermal vents are openings in the ocean floor. Hot water shoots out from the openings. The water that shoots out can be as hot as 700°F!

. . . Quick Cooldown

The super-hot water from the vents quickly cools off. An inch away from the vent the temperature of the water is only 34°F. That's almost freezing

Mussels, clams, shrimp, and snails
call this weird spot home.
Some octopi might swim by.
Some spider crabs might roam.

Lots of different kinds of worms
live here, so take your pick.
Palm worms look like palm trees,
tube worms look like lipstick.

Mineral Snacks

The vents put minerals into the water. Animals that live near the vents need the minerals to survive. One of these minerals is hydrogen sulfide. It smells like rotten eggs!

Eating in, Like a Tube Worm

Giant tube worms that live at the vents have no mouth or stomach. Bacteria live inside the worms. The worms get energy from the bacteria.

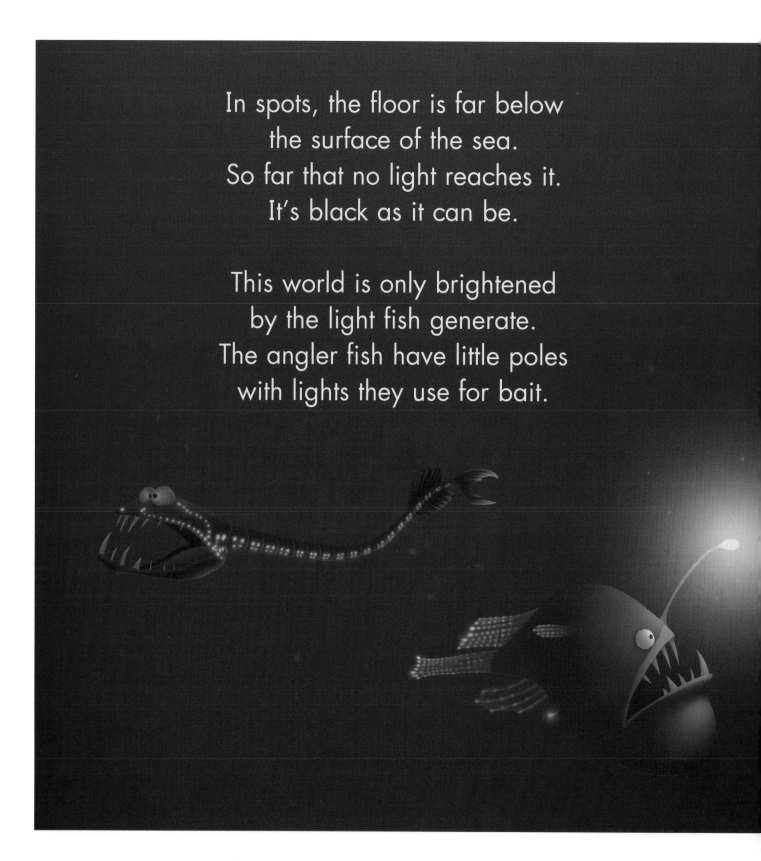

In spots, the floor is far below
the surface of the sea.
So far that no light reaches it.
It's black as it can be.

This world is only brightened
by the light fish generate.
The angler fish have little poles
with lights they use for bait.

Headlights and Taillights

Many deep-sea fish have cells that light up. The lights are found on the fish's body and head. The light is made when special chemicals react.

Loads of Lights

The lights inside fish can help them lure prey. Lights can also help fish find mates. Some fish flash their lights to trick predators.

Other fish have see-through bodies
with lights that flash inside.
Communication? Decoration?
Scientists can't decide.

Under Pressure

It is dark and cold in the deep sea. The water above pushes down with a lot of weight. Scientists used to think that nothing could live there.

I'm So Blue

The lights inside deep-sea fish are almost always blue. Blue light travels far in water. Other colors of light don't travel as far.

19

The ocean bottom isn't flat,
though you might think that's strange.
It has valleys and plateaus
and a giant mountain range.

To reach the ocean's deepest trench
it's straight down seven miles.
But if you want to pay a visit,
it's going to take a while.

Scientists touched the bottom once
in a big French submarine.
It took five hours to drop that far
and there was nothing to be seen.

Too Deep for Me
The Mariana Trench is the deepest place on Earth. Parts of it are almost 7 miles deep.

Diving to the Deep
Scientists went to the bottom of the Mariana Trench in 1960. They dove in a submarine called the *Trieste*. The *Trieste* was built by Auguste Piccard.

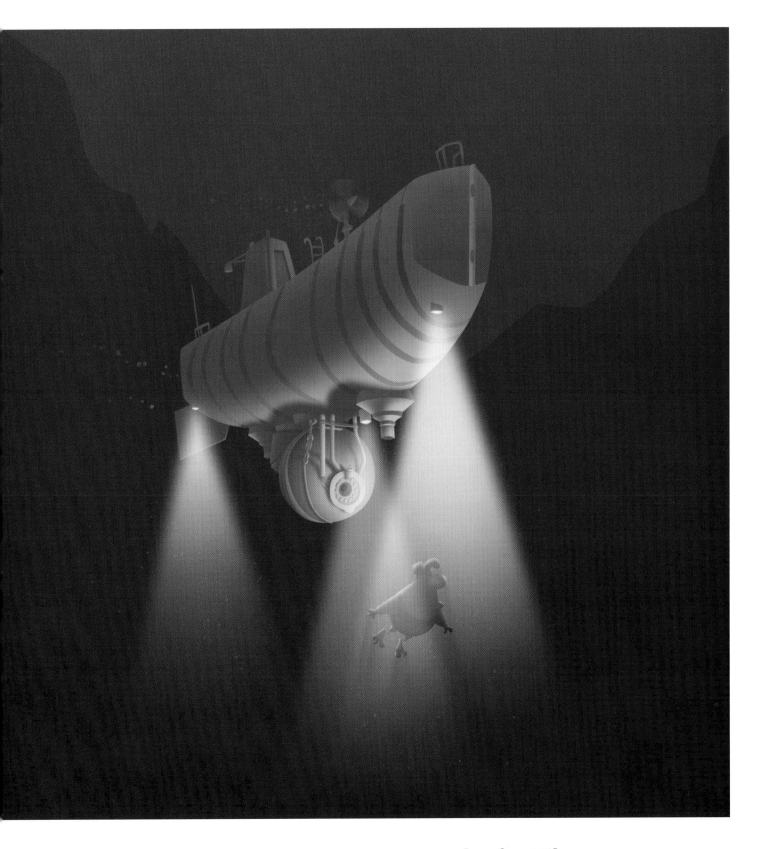

Float Your Boat (or Submarine)

Submarines are filled with air so people inside can breathe. The air also helps the submarine float on the water. Sailors flood parts of the submarine with water to make it dive.

A Heck of a Hike

The longest mountain range on Earth lies under the sea. It is more than 35,000 miles long. It winds its way around the globe. It is called the mid-ocean ridge system.

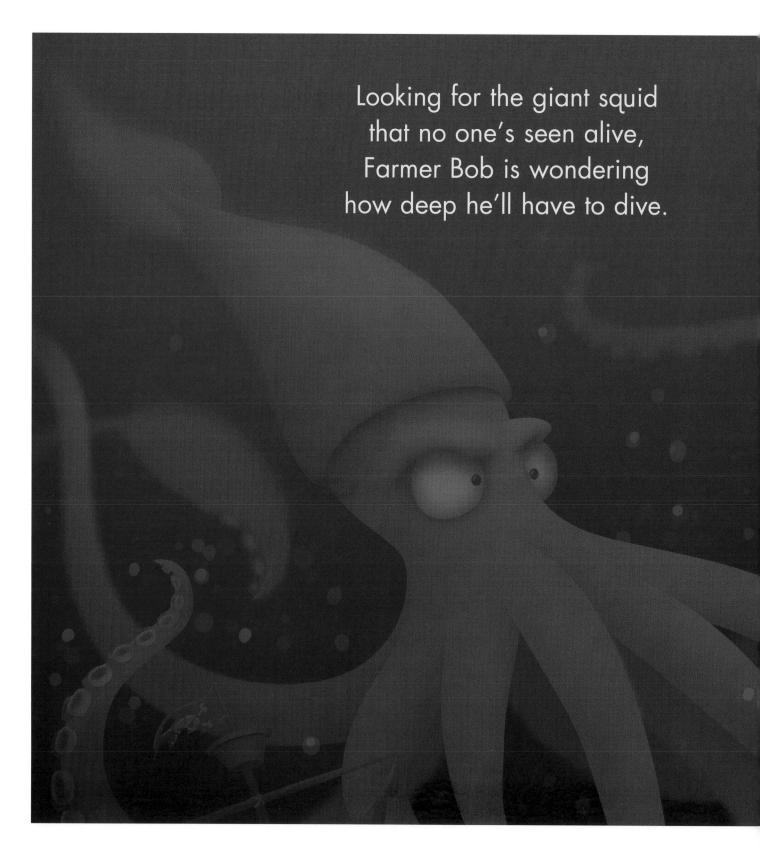

Looking for the giant squid
that no one's seen alive,
Farmer Bob is wondering
how deep he'll have to dive.

What Big Eyes You Have!

Giant squid have huge eyes. They are as big as hubcaps! Giant squid are the only animals with such big eyes.

Big Hug

Giant squid have eight arms and two long tentacles. They use their tentacles to catch prey. They use their beak to eat the food they catch.

Legends say squid were to blame
for sinking sailing ships.
They'd wrap the boats with tentacles,
use suckers for a grip.

59-Foot Squid Song

No one has seen a living giant squid, but dead ones have been found. The largest was 59 feet long!

Legends of the Deep

A legend is a story. It is told so often people think it's true. Sailors told stories about sea monsters. In the stories the monsters attacked ships. These stories became legends.

23

Bob was tired of the deep cold sea
and so he sought relief.
He headed for the warmer waters
around the coral reef.

Coral reefs are actually made
of creatures that have died.
It all sounds very icky,
but gives fish a place to hide.

It's Alive!

Corals are animals related to sea anemones.
Most live in groups called colonies. Coral
animals catch prey with their tentacles.

The Reef of Grief

Only some kinds of coral build reefs. Coral anim
make hard skeletons. The skeletons are left behind
when the animals die. The reef is made of skeleto

Lionfish and tiger sharks
are darting all about.
But if Bob sees a rhinofish,
he'll really give a shout.

A Fishy Tale

Rhinofish aren't real. An artist drew the rhinofish on this page. The artist imagined what the fish would look like. What other strange fish can you imagine?

Tropical Paradise

Coral reefs are found in warm ocean water. The water where coral reefs form isn't very deep. A lot of islands have coral reefs close by.

As Bob swims toward the surface,
he sees a curious sight.
A school of fish has gathered speed.
With fins spread, they all take flight.

When Fish Fly

Flying fish don't "flap their wings" like birds. They swim really fast and jump out of the water. Then they glide through the air like paper airplanes.

Fish Gliders

Flying fish have special fins for gliding. Their front fins are huge. When the fish hold them stiff, the fins are like big wings.

Once they get above the water
these fish just glide and glide.
They can go a quarter mile
with fins stretched out so wide.

Propeller Tail

After a while, a flying fish that's gliding starts to drop back into the water. It dips the end of its tail in the water. It flaps its tail to build speed. Then, it can keep gliding.

Catch Me If You Can!

Other kinds of fish like to catch and eat flying fish. The flying fish jump out of the water to escape. The other fish can't follow!

Farmer Bob has been submerged
for really quite a while.
He pokes his head above the waves
and breaks into a smile.

He spies his surfboard lying on
a nearby island beach.
Then he hears a welcome sound:
a seagull cries out, "SCREECH!"

Farmer Bob is very tired.
He's glad to reach the shore.
He lies down for a little nap
and then he starts to snore.

I Spy an Island

An island is a piece of land with water on all sides. Islands can be found in rivers, in lakes, and in the ocean.

Volcano Island

Some islands are the tops of volcanoes. The island of Hawaii is the top of a volcano. Some other islands are made of coral.

Funny Feet

Gulls have webbed feet. Many birds that spend time in water have webbed feet. They use their webbed feet to paddle in the water.

Would You Like a Pickle with That?

Gulls can drink freshwater or saltwater. They will eat almost any food they can find. Some of the foods they eat are insects, fish, and fruit.

Farmer Bob wakes up confused,
for here are all his chums.
He's on an island far from shore
so where did they come from?

He starts to tell his barnyard friends
what he saw beneath the sea:
the thermal vents, the angler fish,
the cow called manatee.

"That's not what happened, Bob,"
Sam the Ram explains.
"The tenth time you wiped out
you really clonked your brains."

"My adventure—was it all a dream?
That has to be the key.
Next time I'll go to sea for real,
and take all my friends with me."

about the authors and illustrators

Elliott Vanskike
secretly wishes to be a scuba diver. Jacques Cousteau was one of his heroes when he was a child. During the summer, Elliott spent many hours at the pool with his sisters playing a game called "Jacques Cousteau." When he's not dreaming about scuba diving, Elliott loves music, bicycling, and making collages. Elliott lives in Portland, Oregon with his wife and a cat.

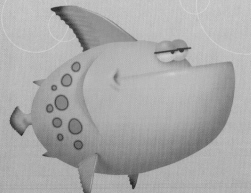

Ray Nelson
likes seafood, especially fish sticks and little crackers shaped like goldfish. He has a big freezer full of fish sticks and a large tub of tartar sauce in his garage. Ray has a pond full of koi fish, but his wife won't let him eat them. Ray is a very good swimmer—when he wears his special water wings.

Ben Adams
lives in a fishbowl. His best friend is a sea monkey named Chip. (Sea monkeys are not really monkeys, they are just called monkeys.) Ben spends a lot of time in the little ceramic castle in his fishbowl, listening to loud music and thinking of different ways to paint fish and barnacles.

Lynnea Eagle
is not a surfer. She has been to the beach. She ate a lot of sand and ocean water as a small child, but she is still not a surfer. Lynnea plays the guitar, and sings Beach Boys songs to her pet betta fish, Diomedes. Together, they hope to start a band and call it "Mad Dog and the Dogfish."